Daddy's Chair

Sandy Lanton

Illustrated by Shelly O. Haas

Kar-Ben Copies, Inc., Rockville, MD

For Jonathan, who misses his daddy very much.
In Memory of Joseph Eisenstein, whose chair was empty much too early.
In Memory of my father, Seymour Fradin, whose influence will always be felt.
—SL

For Phyllis Grode
With special thanks to my mother, John, Jackie, and Glen.
—SOH

Lanton, Sandra.
    Daddy's chair/Sandra Lanton; illustrated by Shelly O. Haas
      p.   cm.
    Summary: When Michael's father dies his family sits shiva, observing the Jewish week of mourning, and remembers the good things about him.
    ISBN 0-929371-51-8 — ISBN 0-929371-52-6 (pbk.) [1. Death—Fiction. 2. Jews—Fiction.] I.
Haas, Shelly O., Ill. II. Title.
    PZ7.L293Dad   1990
[E]—dc20
                                      90-44908
                                         CIP
                                       AC

Published by KAR-BEN COPIES, INC., ROCKVILLE, MD 1-800-4-KARBEN
Printed in the United States of America

"You can't sit there. That's Daddy's chair,"
Michael yelled at his big brother.

Joshua sat down in another chair next to his mother. She was sitting on a low bench.

Michael got his crayons and made a big sign—DADDY. He put it on the chair and went over to his mother. "Only my daddy can sit there," Michael announced. "Nobody else is allowed."

Mommy took Michael on her lap. "Your daddy is dead, Michael," his mother said gently. "You remember the funeral, don't you?"

"Yes," said Michael, "but when he comes back, he's gonna be mad if there's someone else in his chair."

"Your daddy's not coming back. That's what dead means," said Mommy softly.

"Why did he have to die, Mommy?"

"He was very sick, Michael. When Daddy was in the hospital, we had a talk about cancer."

"Yes, about how the bad cells attack the good cells in people's bodies," said Michael. "Like on TV, when the bad guys and the good guys fight."

"Right," said Mommy. "Only on TV the good guys usually win. In real life, it doesn't always work out that way. Sometimes the bad cells take over, no matter what the doctors do."

"And the good guys die," said Michael.

"Yes," said Mommy. "Sometimes good people like your daddy die, no matter how much they want to live. No matter how much their families love them and need them.

No matter how much we would like him to, your daddy isn't going to come back and sit in his chair."

"I know," said Michael, "but Daddy always sat in that chair when we played checkers."

Joshua got the checkerboard out of the cabinet and put it on the ottoman next to Daddy's chair. He opened the box of checkers and placed them on the board. "I can play checkers with you, Michael," he said.

"OK," said Michael. "You can sit in Daddy's chair. But only when we're playing." He took the sign off the chair and sat down on the rug next to the ottoman.

Joshua sat down in Daddy's big leather chair. "Do you want to go first, Michael?" he asked.

After the game, Joshua put the checker set back in the cabinet. Michael put the sign back on Daddy's chair.

All that day and the next, neighbors came to visit.

"Why are you sitting on that little bench?" Michael asked his mother. "Why don't you sit on the couch with me? And why are you wearing your slippers? We have company. Why don't you put your shoes on?"

"When someone dies, the family sits shiva for a week after the funeral," she answered.

"Shiva means seven. For seven days we stay home. We sit on low benches to show that we are feeling low. We don't wear leather shoes or party clothes because they are for happier times. And the torn black ribbon I'm wearing is another symbol of my sadness."

Michael looked around the room. There were platters of food on the dining room table. The house was full of people. Everyone seemed to be talking at once.

"If we're so sad, why are we having a party?" asked Michael.

"It's not a party, Michael," said Mommy. "During shiva, people come to comfort the family. They bring food, so that we don't have to worry about everyday things like cooking."

"We say prayers of mourning, but we also try to celebrate the person's life. People are talking about your daddy. They are remembering the good times, and the nice things he did. Some of the stories are sad, some are funny."

During the next few days, Michael watched over his daddy's chair. He didn't let anyone sit on it. When his Aunt Rachel tried, he said, ''You can't sit there. That's Daddy's chair. Daddy always sat in that chair when he told me stories about when he was little.''

"I can tell you stories about your daddy and me," said Aunt Rachel.

Michael took the sign off the chair. Aunt Rachel sat down and lifted Michael on her lap.

"I remember when I was about your age, and your daddy was even younger. We used to play on the floor of Grandpa's grocery store, while he and Grandma waited on the customers. One time when the store was very busy, we took all the labels off the cans. For weeks, Grandpa had to sell mystery cans. People didn't know if they were buying peaches or green beans."

"My daddy used to tell me that story," said Michael. He leaned his head back against Aunt Rachel.

"Tell me about the mixed nuts."

"OK," said Aunt Rachel. "Another day, Grandma had to make a sign saying MIXED NUTS, because your daddy and I put all the nuts from the nut barrels into one barrel."

"I remember," said Michael. "There were cashews and walnuts…"

"And Brazil nuts and hazelnuts and pistachios and pecans and almonds!" Aunt Rachel added. "At first Grandpa and Grandma were mad, but their customers liked the mixed nuts so well, they started selling them that way on purpose."

"That's enough stories for now," said Michael. He slid off Aunt Rachel's lap and helped her up. Then he put the sign back on Daddy's chair and went over to his mother.

"Daddy always sat in his chair and gave me big bear hugs while we watched TV together," said Michael.

"I'll give you twice as many hugs as before," said Mommy.

"OK, then you can sit in Daddy's chair, too," said Michael. He went over to the chair and took down the sign. Mommy sat down and Michael climbed into her lap. They hugged each other tight. Then Michael climbed down.

"You can go talk to your company now," he said.

He picked up the sign, but put it down again. Instead, he picked up his teddy bear and climbed into the big leather chair.

"And I'll sit here whenever I want to think about my daddy," said Michael.

ABOUT THE AUTHOR

Sandy Lanton, a former teacher, holds a BS in Psychology and an MS in Early Childhood Education from Queens College. She has studied writing, worked as a reporter, and written for *Junior Scholastic, Young American,* and *Hopscotch* magazines. This is her first picture book. Sandy lives in Woodbury, NY with her husband Sy and two kittens. Their children, David and Ruth, are away at college.

ABOUT THE ILLUSTRATOR

Shelly O. Haas has been drawing and painting for most of her life. She received her BFA from The Rhode Island School of Design, and currently lives in Budd Lake, NJ with her husband Gordon, a fine artist, and their son Dillon.
Shelly's first picture book for Kar-Ben, *Grandma's Soup,* was selected as a Sydney Taylor Honor Book for 1989. This is her fourth book for Kar-Ben.